Chef Toussaint

Words By David Miller
Pictures By C.J. Love

This book is a work of fiction. Names, character, places and incidents are the product of the author's imagination or are used fictitiously. Any resemblance to actual events, locales or persons, living or dead, is coincidental.

To Karla, Kelsye, Jihad & Mikalei
Thanks Mom for your love of books.
We miss you, Grammy!

This book is for kids who have forgotten how to dream!

Toussaint L'Ouverture

Have you heard of my world-famous pecan pies? People travel for miles to taste my pies and other foods that I cook and sell to restaurants.

In my family's recipe, we use fresh, organic honey from one of the local beekeepers and handpick pecans from trees on a farm in Fort Valley, Georgia.

Sorry, I am being rude! My name is Toussaint Palmer.

Everybody calls me Chef Toussaint. I am named after the Haitian freedom fighter Toussaint L'Ouverture. I am 9 years old and live in Southwest Atlanta, Georgia, with my mom and dad.

Cooking comes easy for me. I learned how to cook before I could tie my shoes.

Watching my mom and dad cook is one of my favorite things to do. Other kids play basketball while I am cooking in the kitchen or watching the Cooking Channel.

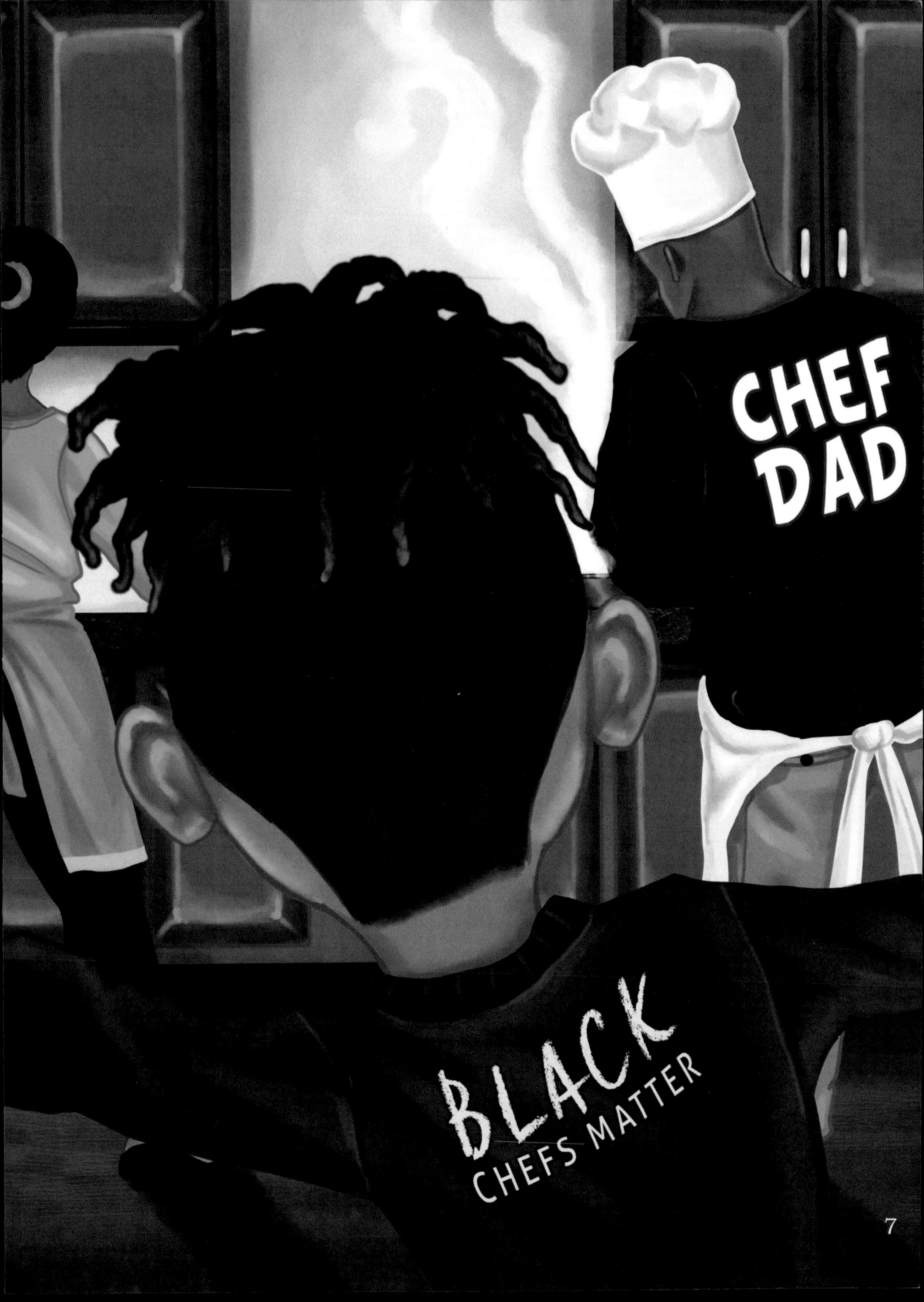
CHEF
DAD
BLACK
CHEFS MATTER

The kitchen is where I make magic.

On some days, I stare out of the window and think about my next masterpiece. Will it be macaroni and cheese, candied sweet potatoes with almonds, or pumpkin pie?

I spend three to four hours in the kitchen during the week and on weekends. It's hard work, but I love cooking, and people enjoy eating my food.

A large brown and black marble table sits in the middle of the kitchen.

Vanilla, nutmeg, cinnamon, basil, curry powder, ginger, and a bunch of other spices sit on the table. Eggs, butter, milk, cheese, onions, parsley, garlic, and mushrooms fill the shelves in the refrigerator.

I keep my large spoons, spatulas, whisks, measuring cups, and an old can opener near the oven.

And we have so many pots, pans, and metal mixing bowls under the table that you would think we own a restaurant downtown.

And these are just a few things I need when I cook.

Nana's Fresh Soul Food

Jackson, Mississippi

We keep Nana's recipes in an old-looking brown box.

Nana was my great-grandmother whose food you could smell from miles away.

Nana and her sisters owned a successful soul food restaurant in Jackson, Mississippi, before moving to Atlanta.

Homemade cornbread, peach cobbler, and banana pudding were some of Nana's favorites.

Nana was best known for her baked salmon with cashews, macaroni and cheese, and potato salad.

I am proud Nana left her recipes for our family so we can continue the tradition of making great food.

15

Sometimes, the neighbors stop by to find out what I am cooking. They say you can smell my collard greens four blocks away on Seventh Avenue.

And when my dad gets his hair cut, the men standing in front of the barbershop tell him how they can smell fried okra coming from our house.

$2 off
FRIDAY SENIOR DAY
FACE & HEAD...

On Friday nights, after I finish my chores, I cook a few large pots of black-eyed peas for several churches nearby. We get fresh onions and garlic from the Johnson Family Farm in McDonough, Georgia.

My dad loves when I make black-eyed peas. I add turkey bacon to give my black-eyed peas more flavor.

CHEF
TOUSSAINT

Details:
h Event (Mon)
Event (Sun)

Delivery Info:
Drop off
Drop off

escription
Black-eyed Peas
Black-eyed Peas

100.00

CHEF
TOUSSAINT

Event Details: Delivery Info:
* Church Event (Mon)   Drop off
Church Event (Sun)   Drop off

Qty   Description
1 Pot   Black-eyed Peas
1 Pot   Black-eyed Peas

Total: __$100.⁰⁰__

Johnson
Family Farm
McDonough, Georgia
Garlic

Johnson
Family Farm
McDonough, Georgia
Onions

And almost every morning, I get up super early to start cooking. I wake up my dad so he can turn on the oven.

My parents are always around when I am cooking. I am not allowed to cook without them being home. Sometimes, I forget I am only nine years old.

Today, I am making four-cheese lasagna.

Johns...
Family Fa...
McDonough, Georg...
Garlic

Lasagna
Noodles

21

Watching my mother cook and learning Nana's recipes, I have become a cooking sensation. While working on my science project for school last weekend, I baked caramel apple fritters for sixteen local restaurants in Atlanta.

My caramel apple fritters were so good that I was invited to appear on the Food Network's, The Best Kid Chefs show last year. I finished in third place.

But today is the big day.

I will participate in the Buckhead Cook-Off. It is a big deal in Atlanta.

Each year, chefs make their favorite desserts and dishes.

Judges take a few days to decide on the winners. The top winner gets their picture on the cover of ATL Magazine and a cash prize.

For me to win would be a big deal. I would be the youngest chef to ever win.

It takes me four hours to make two of my favorites, blueberry pie and grilled sea bass with mango sauce, for the Buckhead Cook-Off. We start at 8 a.m. in a large kitchen.

I love this kitchen. Everything I dreamed about in a kitchen is here. The kitchen has large mixing bowls, giant ovens, and all the spices you can name.

Judges walk by and taste some of the ingredients and ask a bunch of questions.

A photographer from The Atlanta Journal-Constitution, the big newspaper in Atlanta, takes pictures of all the chefs.

Three days later, a few family members and neighbors stop by my house to wait for the results from the judges.

We sit around listening to my parents share stories about Nana and her famous recipes. My mom pulls out the photo album and shows black and white pictures of Nana in the kitchen.

At a few minutes after 7 p.m., my dad's phone rings. After a few minutes, he yells, "Toussaint, you won! You won!"

The room erupts with cheers.

The next day, a bunch of people with cameras prepare me for a photoshoot in the kitchen.

Lights, Camera, Action!

They even try to put makeup on me. But my mom said, "No, he is too young for makeup."

I put on my fresh chef's hat and jacket, and the photographers snap a few pictures of me mixing some eggs in a large metal bowl.

The smile on my face is so big you would have thought I was shooting a toothpaste commercial.

Chef Toussaint
Photoshoot

ATL Magazine

Chef Toussaint
Photoshoot

The next morning, I wake up super early to cook breakfast before school. I love making breakfast for my parents. My dad is up early, watering plants and doing yoga.

He yells, "What's for breakfast?"

And I shout, "Apple cinnamon French toast."

Toussaint L'Ou...

ATL MAGAZINE

Edition # 16 February 2021

Chef
TOUSSAINT

New Recipes

Becoming a master chef

Words By David Miller
Pictures By C.J. Love

I am still excited about being on the cover of a major magazine.

My dad walks inside the house and shows me the front cover of the magazine with my picture on it. "Good Morning America is next."

Black-Eyed Peas

1 pound dried black-eyed peas
1 large onion, chopped
2 tablespoons olive oil
6 garlic cloves, minced
2 bay leaves
1 tablespoon minced fresh thyme
1/4 teaspoon crushed red pepper flakes
1/4 teaspoon pepper
1 carton (32 ounces) vegetable broth
3 packets of Turkey Bacon

Four-Cheese Lasagna

2 cups peeled and diced pumpkin
1 eggplant, sliced into 1/2 inch rounds
5 large tomatoes
1-pint Ricotta Cheese
9 ounces crumbled Feta Cheese
2/3 cup pesto
2 large eggs, beaten
salt and pepper to taste
3 jars of tomato sauce
fresh pasta sheets
1 1/3 cups shredded Mozzarella Cheese
1 cup grated Parmesan cheese

Apple Cinnamon French Toast

3/4 cup butter, melted
1 cup brown sugar
1 teaspoon ground cinnamon
3 medium tart apples, pooled and sliced (about 3 cups)
12 slices white bread
6 large eggs
1 1/2 cups milk
1 teaspoon vanilla extract
1/2 cup maple syrup
1/2 cup dried cranberries

Chef Toussaint's Tips on Teaching Children How to Cook

Parents, here a few great ways to help your children learn and get excited about cooking:

First step: Plan a meal. Sit down with your children to plan a meal.

Second step: Teach your children how to use kitchen appliances. Appliances can include a stove, oven, and dishwasher.

Third step: Help them feel comfortable in the kitchen.

Explore mixing in bowls and measuring sugar, salt, and other ingredients.

Fourth step: Build confidence in the kitchen. Show them how to read recipes by starting with something simple like baking cookies and making a grill cheese sandwich.

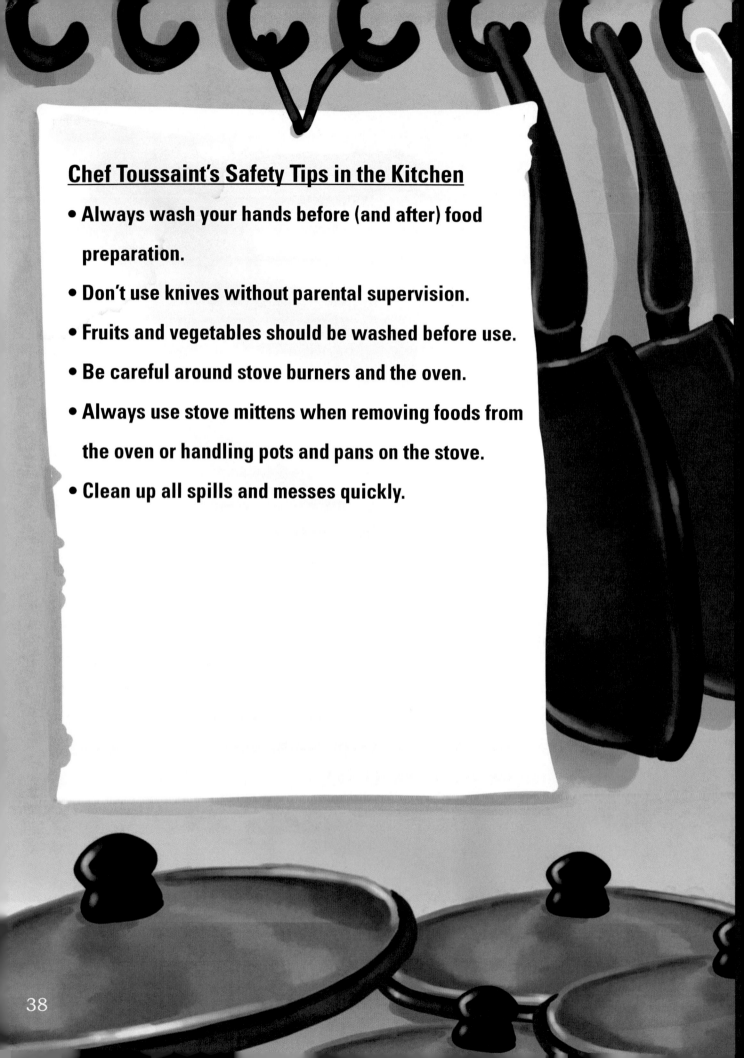

Chef Toussaint's Safety Tips in the Kitchen

- Always wash your hands before (and after) food preparation.
- Don't use knives without parental supervision.
- Fruits and vegetables should be washed before use.
- Be careful around stove burners and the oven.
- Always use stove mittens when removing foods from the oven or handling pots and pans on the stove.
- Clean up all spills and messes quickly.

About the Author

David Miller is the author of several books, including Gabe & His Green Thumb, Brooklyn's Finest: The Greene Family Farm, Khalil's Way, and They Look Like Me (coloring book). Miller's work with youth has been featured in the Baltimore Sun, CNN, PBS, NPR, BBC Magazine, Huffington Post, and a host of other media outlets. He lives in Washington, D.C., with his wife and children. Visit **www.iamdavidmiller.com.**

About the Illustrator

C. J. Love is a graduate of the Maryland Institute College of Art with a Bachelor of Fine Arts degree in Graphic Design. He specializes in illustration, caricatures, mural painting, graphic design, and prototype designs. Visit at **www.clove2design.com.**

40234465R00024